Damián Almaraz

Between Shadows & Stars

Damián Almaraz

Between Shadows & Stars

by

Damián Almaraz

English Edition

Between Shadows & Stars

Introduction

In life, we come across many stories that inspire us, challenge us, and make us reflect on what matters. In this book, we immerse ourselves in one such story, a story of love and sacrifice that transcends the boundaries of time and space.

"Between Shadows and Stars" is more than just a novel; It's an emotional journey that takes us from the glittering halls of high society to the darkest corners of human hearts. At the center of this story are two men, Alexander and Daniel, whose fates are intertwined by an invisible bond that defies all odds.

Throughout these pages, we delve into the world of Alexander and Daniel, two lost souls who find love and redemption in each other's arms. From their first meeting at a glamorous party to the tests of loyalty they face together, we witness the strength and beauty of true love that transcends all barriers.

But as in all great stories, the road to happiness is full of unexpected obstacles and challenges. As Alexander and Daniel struggle to overcome the shadows of the past and face an uncertain future, we are engulfed in a rollercoaster of emotions that leaves us breathless and longing for more.

In "Between Shadows and Stars," the author invites us to reflect on universal themes such as love's power, authenticity's importance, and hope's strength. Through the eyes of Alexander and Daniel, we witness the human being's ability to face adversity with courage and determination and to find light even in the darkest moments.

As we immerse ourselves in this captivating story, we see ourselves reflected in the characters and their struggles, reminding us that love is the most potent force in the universe and that we can overcome any obstacle that comes our way.

So, prepare to embark on an unforgettable journey full of passion, romance, and suspense. In "Between Shadows and Stars," we will discover that even in the darkest corners of the universe, a light of hope and love always shines.

Prologue

On the vast canvas of the universe, where stars dance in the darkness, and fates intertwine in an intricate fabric of time and space, lies a story of love and redemption that transcends the barriers of time and distance. It's a story of two lost souls who find their way home in each other's arms, bravely facing adversity and finding the light even in the darkest times.

At the heart of this story are Alexander and Daniel, two men whose fates are intertwined by an invisible bond that defies all odds. Raised in opposite worlds but united by a common yearning for acceptance and love, they meet in a chance encounter that will change their lives forever.

From their first meeting at a party filled with lights and laughter to the tests of loyalty they face together, we witness the power of true love to heal and transform even the darkest circumstances. Throughout their journey, we are immersed in a world of passion, romance, and suspense, where each twist and turn takes us deeper into the abyss of their hearts and reminds us of the beauty and miracle of true love.

But as in all great stories, the road to happiness is full of unexpected obstacles and challenges. As Alexander and Daniel struggle to overcome the shadows of the past and face an uncertain future, we are engulfed in a rollercoaster of emotions that leaves us breathless and longing for more.

These pages explore universal themes such as love's power, authenticity's importance, and hope's strength. Through the eyes of Alexander and Daniel, we face our struggles and triumphs, reminding us that although life may be difficult and the path uncertain, there is always light in the darkness and hope in the human heart.

So, my dear reader, be prepared to embark on an unforgettable journey full of passion, romance, and suspense. Because in the vast universe of love, there are no boundaries or borders, and there is always someone out there waiting for you with open arms and a heart full of love - a story of Alexander

Between Shadows & Stars

Damián Almaraz

and Daniel, a story of love and redemption that you will never forget.

Between Shadows & Stars

Dedication:

This book is dedicated with love and admiration to the LGBTQ+ community, whose stories of courage, resilience, and love have inspired millions worldwide. Through your struggles and triumphs, you have shown that love knows no boundaries or boundaries and that we deserve to be loved and accepted just as we are.

This book is for those who have faced adversity with courage and determination, fought for equality and justice, and found love in the most unexpected places. May these pages remind you that you are not alone, that there is hope in the darkest times, and that there will always be someone willing to love you just as you are.

May this story of love and redemption bring you comfort and hope, reminding you that each of us deserves to find happiness and true love in this life. Because in the vast universe of love, no matter who you are or where you come from, there is always someone out there waiting for you with open arms and a heart full of love.

With love and gratitude,

Damián Almaraz

Damián Almaraz

Table of Contents

Encounter in the Dark 13

Secrets in the Shadows......................19

Confessions in the Night 24

Loyalty Tests....................................30

The Gift of Love 35

The Road to Recovery......................39

An uncertain future 43

Between Shadows & Stars

Damián Almaraz

Encounter in the Dark

Between Shadows & Stars

In the heart of the city that never sleeps, on a night where the stars seem to twinkle with a secret conspiracy, fate weaves its invisible threads among the glow of a party full of lights and laughter. In that labyrinth of glamour and appearances, two souls destined to meet through the crowd, their paths intertwined by a design more significant than themselves.

With his elegant bearing and captivating gaze, Alexander walks with the confidence of someone raised between luxury and power. His eyes scan the room, searching for something he can't yet name, a longing that pulsates deep within him, waiting to be released by a chance encounter with a stranger.

Daniel, with his shy smile and eyes full of curiosity, enters the party with the naivety of someone who has not yet discovered that the world has secrets. His steps lead him down an unknown path, but his heart beats to the rhythm of an ancient melody, a love song waiting to be sung by someone he does not yet know.

And then, amid the crowd, their gazes meet in a flash of mutual recognition, as if the universe had conspired to bring them together at that very moment. In that brief instant of connection, time stands still, and the noise of the party fades into the echo of their hearts beating in unison, like two perfect notes meeting in the harmony of destiny.

Between Shadows & Stars

Without words or gestures, they approach each other, attracted by a magnetic force enveloping them in an invisible embrace, sealing their encounter with a silent pact that only the universe can understand. And so, in the dead of night, two lost souls find their home in each other's arms, beginning a love story that will transcend time and space.

Time seems to stand still as Alexander and Daniel immerse themselves in each other's gaze, lost in a sea of emotions that envelop them in a bubble of intimacy. The conversations around them fade into the background, leaving only the sound of their heartbeats synchronized in a perfect rhythm of collaboration and understanding.

Daniel's smile is like a beacon in the darkness, lighting the way to an unknown world that Alexander longs to explore. In every gesture, every word whispered in his ear, he finds a reason to believe in the power of love and authentic connection.

For his part, Alexander awakens in Daniel a deep desire to be seen and accepted as he is, without masks or pretensions. In his eyes, he finds a reflection of his soul, a light that guides him to the truth of who he is.

Together, they venture into the most intimate corners of their inner worlds, sharing dreams, fears, and longings with a disarming honesty. Each confession strengthens the bond they are building, woven with the threads of trust and vulnerability.

Between Shadows & Stars

As the night progresses and the party ends, Alexander and Daniel are reluctant to leave the refuge they have created in each other. In that magical moment between day and night, they say goodbye with the unspoken promise of a new dawn, where their story is just beginning to be written.

Damián Almaraz

Secrets in the Shadows

Between Shadows & Stars

Damián Almaraz

The sun rises above the horizon, painting the sky with golden and pink hues that herald the start of a new day. As the world awakens around them, Alexander and Daniel are plunged into a whirlwind of emotions that drag them even deeper into the abyss of their connection.

With every thought they share, every furtive glance they exchange, the bonds that bind them strengthen as if they were destined to meet at this precise time and place. However, amid the euphoria of their growing love, a dark shadow lurks that threatens to obscure their budding brilliance.

Between Shadows & Stars

The secrets they hold, the walls they have built around their hearts, stand as invisible barriers between them, preventing their love from fully blossoming. Alexander, accustomed to hiding his true self behind a mask of perfection and control, fears that the truth of his sexual orientation could jeopardize everything he has built.

For his part, Daniel carries with him the weight of a childhood marked by bigotry and rejection, afraid to reveal his true self to a world that has never been kind to him. Despite his undeniable attraction for Alexander, he wonders if he can ever be brave enough to leap to freedom and authenticity.

Amid their internal struggles, they find solace in each other's arms, sharing moments of tenderness and complicity that transport them to a world where time stands still and worries fade away. In every stolen kiss and gentle caress, they find a haven to be themselves without fear of judgment or condemnation.

But even in the brief happiness they find in each other, the shadow of their secrets threatens to overshadow their love. In awkward silence, evasive glances, and unspoken words, they feel the weight of lies and disappointment creeping in between them, pulling them apart when they most need to be together.

And so, in the heat of their growing passion, they face a crossroads that could change their lives forever. Will they have the courage to face the truth and open their hearts completely, or will they succumb to the weight of secrets that threaten to destroy them from within? Only time will tell, as their love is tested in destiny's crucible.

Damián Almaraz

Confessions in the Night

Between Shadows & Stars

The moon shines overhead, illuminating Alexander and Daniel's path as they venture into the depths of the night, exploring the darkest corners of their souls with a bravery that only love can inspire. In the stillness of the darkness, they find themselves enveloped in a silent embrace, their hearts beating in unison in a rhythm of collaboration and understanding.

In this moment of shared intimacy, the walls they have built around their hearts begin to crumble, yielding to the irresistible force of truth. With each shared sigh, each looks laden with meaning; they open up to each other in a way they have never experienced before, revealing layers of vulnerability and authenticity that connect them on a deeper level than the physical.

With his intense gaze and trembling voice, Alexander dares to confess the weight he's carried on his shoulders for so long, the secret hidden behind a façade of perfection and control. With tears in his eyes and his heart in his throat, he reveals the truth about his sexual orientation, fearing Daniel's reaction to this intimate and personal revelation.

Daniel listens silently, his eyes filled with compassion and understanding, as Alexander emotionally undresses. He shares the fears and doubts that have plagued his mind since childhood. Instead of judging or rejecting him, he wraps him in a comforting embrace, offering him the gift of unconditional acceptance and unwavering love.

And then, it's Daniel's turn to open his heart and reveal the demons he's been battling in the dark, the invisible scars he's carried with him since he was just a scared, lonely child. With a trembling voice and sweaty hands, he confesses his deepest secrets, revealing his identity and his battles in his search for acceptance and love.

Alexander listens intently, his eyes filled with wonder and admiration as Daniel shares his story with a courage that takes his breath away. In that moment of intimate connection, they realize that they are not alone in their struggles but share an indestructible bond that transcends the barriers of time and space.

As the night progresses and the stars twinkle in the sky, Alexander and Daniel are immersed in an embrace that envelops them in a sense of peace and fulfillment they have never known before. In that magical moment between darkness and dawn, they promise each other that they will never again hide the truth of who each of them is and that they will always be honest and truthful with each other, no matter the consequences.

And so, in the silence of the night, two lost souls find their way back home, finding love and redemption in each other's arms. As the new day looms, they know their journey is just beginning. Still, they are ready to face any challenge together, armed with the power of true love and the strength of their eternal connection.

Damián Almaraz

Loyalty Tests

Between Shadows & Stars

Damián Almaraz

The sun rises above the horizon, illuminating the world with its warm glow as Alexander and Daniel soak in the first rays of the new day. With hearts full of hope and determination, they face the challenges ahead, ready to face any obstacle that life throws them together.

However, fate has other plans, and they soon face a test of loyalty that will test the limits of their love and commitment to each other. When Alexander receives the devastating diagnosis of chronic kidney disease, his world reels, leaving him dazed and desperate to find a solution.

Between Shadows & Stars

Amid uncertainty and fear, Daniel becomes his rock, his unwavering support in times of need. He holds you with love and compassion every step of the way, reminding you that together, you can overcome any challenge.

But when doctors announce that Alexander urgently needs a kidney transplant, the reality of the situation becomes even more heartbreaking. Despite the compatibility tests, no available donors are on the waiting list, leaving Alexander with few options and an uncertain future.

That's when Daniel makes the most difficult decision of his life, offering Alexander the most precious gift he can give: his kidney. With his heart in his throat and his eyes welling with tears, he volunteers to undergo the surgery, knowing he is risking his own life for the man he loves.

For Alexander, Daniel's gesture is an act of pure, selfless love, a reminder of the strength of their bond and the depth of their connection. With tears of gratitude and admiration in his eyes, he accepts the gift of life that Daniel offers him, promising himself to honor his sacrifice by living each day with gratitude and love in his heart.

And so, amidst the darkness of illness and uncertainty, Alexander and Daniel's love shines like a beacon of hope and redemption, lighting the way to a future full of promise and possibility. As they prepare to face the surgery that will change their lives forever, they know that their love is more vital than any adversity and that together, they can overcome any challenge that comes their way.

Damián Almaraz

The Gift of Love

Between Shadows & Stars

The day of surgery comes with a mixture of anxiety and hope filling the air around you. In the hospital waiting room, Alexander and Daniel cling to each other, their hands clasped like an unbreakable bond that binds them together amid uncertainty and fear.

Time seems to pass in slow motion as they wait for news on the progress of the surgery, every passing minute filled with agony and anticipation. Amidst the heavy silence, their thoughts turn to the uncertain future that awaits them, wondering if they can ever regain the normalcy they once knew.

Finally, the surgeon enters the room, his face severe and sad as he reports on the operation's success. With a sigh of relief, Alexander and Daniel hug each other tightly, tears of gratitude and joy flowing freely down their cheeks.

The gift of love that Daniel has given Alexander is more than a kidney; It is a powerful symbol of their commitment and devotion to each other. In that moment of deep connection, they realize the depth of their love and the strength of their bond, strengthened by adversity and united in victory over illness.

As they recover in the warmth of their home, surrounded by love and support from friends and family, Alexander and Daniel realize that their story is far from over. Despite the challenges they faced in the past and the obstacles they may still face, they know they have the power of love on their side, guiding them through the dark times and leading them into the light.

As the sun sets over the horizon and the world plunges into darkness, Alexander and Daniel hug each other tightly, knowing that together, they can overcome any challenge that comes their way. With the gift of love as their guide, they are ready to face the future with courage and determination, knowing that as long as they are together, there is nothing they cannot overcome.

Damián Almaraz

The Road to Recovery

Between Shadows & Stars

Alexander and Daniel's home becomes a sanctuary of love and healing as they both recover from the surgery that changed their lives forever. Each day, they cling to each other with renewed determination, finding comfort and strength in their love.

The days become a mix of small victories and unexpected challenges. Still, together, they face every obstacle with courage and determination. With the help of their loved ones, they find the strength to keep going, knowing that as long as they're together, there's nothing they can't overcome.

For Alexander, recovery is a constant reminder of the fragility of life and the importance of living each day with gratitude and love in your heart. Every step he takes, every moment he shares with Daniel, is a gift he doesn't take for granted, a reminder of the beauty and fragility of human life.

For Daniel, donating his kidney to Alexander is an act of love he will never forget. As he recovers from surgery, he reflects on the meaning of sacrifice and the importance of giving himself to those he loves. In Alexander's arms, he finds the peace and fulfillment he's been searching for all his life, knowing that together, they can overcome any challenge that comes their way.

As the days and weeks pass, life slowly returns to normal for Alexander and

Daniel. They immerse themselves in the daily grind with gratitude and joy, knowing that every moment together is a precious gift they won't take for granted.

And while the future is still uncertain and full of unknown challenges, they know they can face whatever life throws at them as long as they're together. With love as their guide and strength, they are ready to face the future with courage and determination, knowing their love is more vital than any adversity.

Damián Almaraz

An Uncertain Future

Between Shadows & Stars

Damián Almaraz

Time marches on, and the seasons change. Alexander and Daniel face an uncertain future full of possibilities and challenges. Although their love is strong and their bond is unbreakable, they know the road ahead will not be without difficulties.

The shadows of the past still lurk in the darkest corners of their minds, reminding them of the obstacles they've overcome together and the demons they may still have to face in the future. As they face the uncertainties of everyday life, they cling to each other with renewed determination, knowing that together, they can overcome any challenge that comes their way.

But even amid hardship and challenges, moments of joy and happiness light their path and remind them of the beauty and miracle of true love. In the little things of everyday life, they find the magic and wonder that unites them, reminding them of the power of love to heal and transform even in the darkest circumstances.

They know more trials and tribulations will be ahead as they move forward into the future together. Still, moments of joy and happiness await them on the horizon. With love as their guide and strength, they are ready to face whatever life throws at them, knowing that as long as they are together, there is nothing they can't overcome.

Between Shadows & Stars

As the sun sets on the horizon and the world plunges into darkness, Alexander and Daniel hug each other tightly, knowing that their love is more vital than any adversity and that they can overcome whatever life throws at them. With the future full of promise and possibility, they are ready to face whatever fate throws at them, knowing that as long as they are together, they can face anything that comes their way.

Damián Almaraz

Between Shadows & Stars

Damián Almaraz

Between Shadows & Stars